Blake

THE FOUND BY YOU SERIES: BOOK SIX

VICTORIA H SMITH

St. Albert's Hospital
El Paso, Texas
Four years ago

One

ANN

I WASN'T USED to good things happening to me, a lifetime of living for others when living for *myself* should have been the priority. They'd been long and sometimes hard lessons learned, but in the end, they'd been my struggle to make. I'd taken the burden of them with me for far too long, and I was finally starting to see relief of their heavy weight in my time and life ahead. I started to feel their liberation here, in this place.

I'd worked in St. Albert's Hospital for a few years now. They'd been short, wonderful years for me and each day my heart selfishly hoped for something it really didn't want. I didn't want to see... *him* again.

Because that meant he was here.

He'd be here amongst the sick and suffering. He'd be here amongst the dying. In the past several days, he almost did die. His heart had given out, his big, strong heart I remembered.

We had not even two days spent together. We only had hours in which a lifetime of memories could be formed. I knew because I took them with me. I took them long after my heart beat for another however faint it'd been. I'd chosen a different path in the end. Perhaps, the wrong path. Perhaps not, but if a lesson was learned in the end was a choice ever the wrong path? The answer to this question I was unsure of. I never had all the answers. I never knew all the right things to do. Like was it right for me to linger in his room long past the hours of his family? Was it *right* for me to make myself scarce and not let him see me?

Was it right for my heart to still beat in the way it did when he was around?

I never knew the answers to these questions. I never knew what was right. I just remembered what it felt like to be in his energy.

"Anita?"

As well as how my lungs felt too big for my chest when I realized he remembered me too.

I'd slipped that day. I didn't come in when he'd been sleeping or busy with his family. I stayed long past when I should.

He was different now, no more a man a few years shy of a boy. He'd been so sick when he'd come in, his skin pale and lips a soft pink, but no longer the case.

Turning, I saw the large and encompassing build of a man, his skin stressed and labored from age but matured. He had matured from his defined jawline to his impressive frame, his blond locks and goatee lacking the luster of youth but not much other than that changed. He was still Blake, the kindness there beneath those pale blue eyes.

"Ann."

His eyes let in more light, as he relaxed into my name. It'd been as if it'd brought him peace.

As if *I* brought him peace.

My chart, his chart, hit my hip and when I came to him from across his hospital room we simply looked at each other, stared *into* each other. It was as if we were looking for the past.

Or maybe we were looking for the future.

RURAL TEXAS, USA
The Summer of 1985

Two

BLAKE

"This seat isn't taken by chance... is it?"

The clatter of the diner cutlery and general banter faded off behind a feminine voice.

My hand smoothed across the charcoal sketch I'd been working on for the majority of my lunch break, looking up to find the deepest, darkest eyes cast in my direction.

She was... beautiful and that was honest to God the first thought I had about the woman standing by my table.

Lashes with the thickest curl framed almond-shaped eyes, her subtle blinks like a peek into the abyss of her liquid-brown irises. She pushed back full ringlets of bushy curls from her hollowed cheeks of the sharpest height and I'd never seen anything like them outside of movies or the magazines the guys at the quarry passed around the job. The content of them wasn't always tasteful but the girls in the centerfolds always had high cheekbones.

This girl had them too, the pink band in her hair matched the top she wore that spread out in a V-shape above her chest and exposed the rich tone of her mahogany skin. Staring, I pulled my journal back.

"Ma'am?" I questioned, not really understanding what she'd asked me. I was at a booth, no free chairs to take or anything.

Her lashes proceeded in a rapid blink once my voice hit the air and I noticed a subtle smile spread out on her full lips when her head tilted away.

A soft but present, "Ma'am...?" hummed so light from her lips I figured the existence of the word hadn't been meant for me, and when she pushed the halo of her big hair from her eyes, she shook her head a little.

"I really am in Texas," she said, more to herself than me and I indeed could confirm that for her, myself born and raised in this small town outside of El Paso.

I never really had a reason to leave the area quite honestly and this one, well she looked far from here. Like a polished penny in a creek, she stood out from this place, her brown boots pretty like her eyes and shining bright with the skirt she chose to go with it all. It bowed out over the thickness of her hips and accentuated the trim shape of her waist as it pushed up to full breasts.

These were all things I tried not to notice, wanting to be a gentleman but the way she looked at me made all those obvious observations I noticed about her hard to ignore.

She was looking at me like a new penny too.

Perhaps realizing that, her lashes flashed away, those high cheekbones going round with her grin.

"I'd like to share a table with you if I could," she said, pushing all that hair away from her face again. When she did, the diner's light showed brightly through the massive curls around her, the tone of her hair actually more of a light brown.

Her lashes flashed up. "I never do this, ask to sit with people I don't know, but this place is rather busy."

I lifted my head, suddenly aware we weren't the only two

people in the room, the diner's patrons both at tables and the counter. Some had even taken standing as an option to sip their coffee and I wasn't surprised. The diner was a direct line to most of the businesses in town. That's why I chose to eat here on lunch, the location a hop and skip away from the rock quarry.

"Could I sit with you? Only if you have room of course. I've been traveling a long time."

The bag appeared behind her like an apparition, the duffle on wheels large and jam-packed to the full extent of its bindings. It went with her outfit too, a light pink like peonies in the wind.

She smelled as such when I told her she could join me, my nod, then smile following that flowery smell. Her scent was an array of many, like a full and constant meadow in the air normally thick with workers and flapjacks. For the lunch hour, the short-order cooks had cheese sandwiches on the grill and I moved the stuff across the table for my companion.

She was a pretty little thing and kind of bashful, as she wouldn't keep my eye contact for nothing. Making it easy for her, I waved down Maybelle so she could take the girl's order. She'd come and gone from my table, my plate of chicken fried steak cleaned long ago, so her eyes went wide when she noticed me gesturing to her. She'd already given me my check, but despite doing that she came over, her hands on her hips. A square tag reading "Maybelle" fastened to her wide bosom and she grinned at me upon stopping by my booth.

"Hungry again already, Blake?" she questioned, jostling me like she always did. She'd been serving me for years at this place, us all in here really well acquainted since this was a small town.

"I'm all right, Ms. Maybelle," I admitted. My momma's influence to regard all women senior to me properly was strong within me. I missed my momma a lot, both she and my pop gone too soon. They passed in a car accident shortly after I'd entered high school, my great-grandmama raising me into a man in the end.

I opened my hands to the woman across from me, the one who now held my gaze with a soft smile.

Unnerved a bit by the sudden attention, I scratched the back of my neck with my finger.

"She, uh... hasn't ordered."

The attention gratefully moved away from me and to the girl, my hand moving to my lap as I watched her order. She wanted a lemonade and an iced tea, wanting to mix the two herself. I thought it'd been kind of a sweet order, different and all that. Before Maybelle left she offered me another coffee, which I took her up right away on. I had a long day at the quarry yet, my days there some of the longest before I clocked out.

I'd been working there since I graduated high school, many of us had. It was a big place with lots of jobs, easy decision for me.

My hand moved across the table, the girl with the big brown eyes and cheekbones from those centerfolds looking at me. Fluffing her curls restlessly with a hand, she managed to make them bushier. Girls around here did that as well.

"Your name is Blake?" she asked me, her framed eyelashes covering her eyes a little and I felt the extent of rude for not introducing myself right away. I guess things had happened quickly.

"Uh, yeah," I mumbled, unfortunately always mumbling. My momma used to get on me for sounding like I had cotton in my mouth. She had me in speech therapy for a time but I must have frustrated her with all that by not getting better because at some point she never kept me going with it.

My fingers moved on the table.

"And you, um...?"

Her eyes did this thing, crinkling hard in the corners yet soft at the same time. The look had my insides feeling all bunched up and I wondered how much of my lack of proper speech had anything to do with my actual capabilities.

"Ann, well, Anita," she told me from under her hair. Moving, her curls bounced all over the place and my mind moved with the images of what they'd do when she danced, how her smile would be *while* she danced.

She shrugged. "I'm Ann. Short for Anita, but yes, Ann's fine."

Ann.

I liked that, both of the versions, and I nodded. Her gaze studied me again and I really wasn't used to people paying that much attention to me day to day. I never gave them a reason to I guess, keeping to myself and doing my work.

But for some reason, she fixed in my direction, her dark eyes shifting from that of my clean-shaven face, neck, and lower. Her vision wandered over my shoulders, then across my chest, the name tag "Blake" I knew to be covered in the debris and aftermath from working countless days in a rock quarry. I brushed most of it off before coming to lunch but never had been good about getting all of it.

Her sudden appraisal of how I looked had me fidgeting, this girl, clean as a shiny whistle, in front of me. Her smart clothes and city looks were a far cry from the dust and grime that covered an old set of work bibs and dirty-blond hair that was always just a little too long. It fell unruly just past my ears and no doubt had just as much dust as my bibs. Like my clothing I always brushed off before leaving my job for lunch but I wasn't kempt in the slightest.

At least not like her.

"You're from the city?" I questioned, hoping she'd stop her gaze for a time and I could settle my nerves a little. I didn't run nervous usually. I guess today was different.

My change of direction had her focusing on something other than me for a moment and when her drinks came she mixed them, choosing to slide her lemonade into the iced tea. She ordered one of the diner's grilled cheese sandwiches before Maybelle went ahead to her other tables. I smiled when she used her straw to stir her lemonade-tea combination. I recalled that mix being called an Arnold Palmer.

She smiled.

"What makes you think I'm from the city?" she asked, not looking at me and my finger moved in the direction of her bag on the floor.

"Well, you said you traveled," I said. "And then there's your accent."

It rang up north, far north and away from here.

The crinkling deepened in her eyes and her lips twitched up. She nodded.

"New York," she said and like I believed far from here. She grinned. "But I'm traveling from California. Just graduated from UCLA, heading back home now."

A college girl, talk about something shiny and new.

And definitely far from here.

I never went to college, no reason for me to. We all just kind of got lost here after high school, expected to start jobs and live our lives. Many of my friends and classmates got married right away and settled in. I figured that'd end up being me too when it all panned out. When the time was right for all that, that was.

"The train I was on actually had a layover here," Ann continued on. Her straw darkened with a sip of her Arnold Palmer. "So I guess I'm a Texas resident for the next day or so. I plan to find a motel after eating something. I just wanted to rest for a little bit I guess. The train was hot and I'm tired."

"And you're traveling by it to New York?" I asked, eyes widening. "You're not traveling by plane?"

Lord knew it'd be easier. She'd get to her destination in hours and not the days such a trip would take.

Ann didn't answer right away and I realized rather quickly I put my foot in something I had no business doing. My finger shot behind my neck and I restlessly moved my nail bed against the back.

"I, uh…" I mumbled again, my gaze sliding away. "I'm sorry. Wasn't my place. I guess I'm just curious."

In the end, invasively so, but if Ann was put off by what I said she didn't show it.

If anything, she only smiled again.

"No, you're right," she said, her dark skin hinting at a blush across her chest where the tone was more fair. It crept up the side of her neck and her hand went there, her delicate fingers painted in the same pink as her bag and top.

"I'm just scared of planes," she admitted and just about half her drink went down with her sip. Her confession had her bashful and moving, I let her know she didn't need to be.

"I guess we both are," I admitted too, but not as brave I gazed out the window to my hometown. I'd been restricted by the invisible walls of this place, old shops and local businesses around the destiny I chose. I never saw fit to leave, but if I had the desire I believed I would see the world. I just needed a reason to see it for.

Ann was suddenly quiet, but then again, so was I. My gaze sliding, I caught her in another one of her fixated stares, but this time she studied something beneath my hand.

The moleskin notebook lay opened, and having no time, I couldn't push it away before she noticed. She'd already seen it and I hadn't wanted to be rude by removing it quickly.

Noticing *I noticed* her staring at it, she tried to pretend she hadn't been doing just that—staring. This had been made easier when Maybelle chose that exact opportunity to arrive with her food but even after the plate had been presented and the waitress gone, the existence of the moment rang loud between us. I still had my hand on the notebook.

And it was still open with the contents inside.

"You're an artist," she chose to say, nibbling on her grilled cheese. She swallowed. "I had no idea I was sitting across from one."

No sarcasm ran in her voice and our friendly banter up to this point gave no relationship in which such joking would be appropriate I supposed.

Her seriousness, her genuine seriousness about what she said regarding my sketching had my hand moving across the pad. Left-handed, I always caught charcoal on the underside.

"They're just things I fool with," I said, shrugging off the pages I worked on literally every spare moment I had. I shook my head, strands of my hair sticking to my brow. I pushed them away. "I like to sketch when I have the time."

And that's one thing I did have here. I had time after hours and even on the clock though I made sure my boss never knew. The pad was small enough to keep in my coveralls and my pencils never took up much space.

Ann swallowed another bite of sandwich she ate and as her gaze kept sliding I figured it was rude to not show her.

My fingers lifted from the soft and detailed lines of a dollhouse I imagined, the magazines of cover girls and pinups not the only ones that circulated around the quarry. Sometimes I was fortunate enough to come across a wood-working magazine. That's where I'd seen the dollhouse. It'd been one of a much similar design and once I figured out the issues I had with it, I created it. Two stories, it even had a little garage, something cute a kid would like probably.

Rather hesitant, shy like she'd been so far, Ann moved her body in the direction of the sketch. Her subtle scent moved with her and I wondered how well she could take *me* in. After all, I'd been greedily indulging in her, how good she smelled.

Sitting back, I moved so she wouldn't gain the opportunity, but I lifted my fingers enough so she could see.

"This is beautiful," she said, smile moving wide across her full lips. She had some of the fullest, a gloss there I was close enough to see now. She bit her lip. "More than just dabbling here and there."

"Not much more," I told her, my fingers lifting higher. She could see the full house now. My jaw moved. "They're things I made or want to make."

"Wait. You make these things?"

I had her attention now and I knew it the moment she moved closer, her wide array of exuberant curls just inches from me. I thought about things that probably weren't proper as some of them reached out and wafted the smell of sweet shampoos and other stuff girls added to their hair to make it soft-looking and bouncy. I envisioned things like touching those curls and watching my fingers disappear in the thickness.

"Not this in particular," I said swallowing back the urge. I faced the sketch. "This is one I want to make, but these I have made."

Since she seemed interested I showed her, starting with the matching rocking chairs I constructed for the reverend and his wife. I'd made several of these, each different with subtle elements I thought of on the fly.

Ann's hand lifted with the pages, like each one flipped she wanted to reach out and touch. She did touch one, my best work I considered.

The pulpit I got to see every Sunday at church, the entire congregation around it and settling pride in my chest each service I witnessed it.

"These are your dreams," Ann said and like something she'd spoken before I thought not meant for me. It'd been so light when she spoke the word and had I not guessed she'd been from the city I would have known right there. She spoke of dreams.

She spoke of accomplishments outside of this place.

I could say nothing more than, "I guess," I felt my default. It was easy to "guess" or "suppose." It was simpler.

Ann dampened her soft lips, something I surmised about them. They had to be soft, so full and puckered.

"I had a notebook like this once," she admitted sitting back, but then went shy again. "But it was nothing like yours inside. I put stupid things in it. Things like eat an entire bowl of ice cream with as many flavors as I could think of or just have the best day ever whatever that means."

Her head shook as she thought of that last one.

She grinned. "I even wanted to shout as loud and as obnoxious as I could from the top of the Empire State Building. I put that in there too. Like I said, stupid things."

They didn't sound stupid. If anything they sounded freeing, liberating.

Playing with the edge of my notebook, I looked up at her.

"Why the Empire State Building?" I questioned, then felt as if I was kind of getting in her business again. I shook my hair out. "You don't have to tell me or anything. I just wondered."

She actually looked grateful that I wasn't finding this whole topic of conversation weird or anything, indulging me when she pushed her hands on the table.

"Because it's possible," she said simply. "Because it's there and I'm sure a lot of people haven't done it. It also happened to be the highest place I could think of at the time. It just made sense."

It did make sense and like I said, sounded incredibly freeing.

Ann's expression changed as she looked at me, her big

curls pushing across her high cheekbones, she fell back in the booth.

"Let's talk about something else, please," she said, the tops of her shoulders bouncing a little with her laugh. "You're probably regretting letting me sit here."

In fact, quite the opposite. Though, I didn't share that with her or anything. I actually liked sitting with her. I liked talking with her about nothing, about everything.

My hand moved on my notebook and her chin tipped out in its direction.

"But those are beautiful," she said. "It'd be amazing if I could do something like that."

"But then you wouldn't find it so cool," I said. "And I wouldn't be able to impress you."

I had no idea why I said it and immediately looked away after. I found myself saying things... sharing things like my designs with her when I normally wouldn't with anyone. I had no reason to. Just my hobby and not really concerning anyone else.

Her lips moved and I found myself watching them, attracting my way to them like a honeybee to a fragrant flower. Ann might have said something in that moment. I wanted her to, but Maybelle came with her bill.

The city girl thanked her, paying her right then and there and the tip must have been gracious because Maybelle thanked her profusely with a blush on her big cheeks.

Ann simply lifted a hand. I guess this was all second nature to her. I wondered where she came from, not where she lived but *where* she came from and who she was. We didn't have a lot of time today, the limits of the time apparent when she sat up, reaching an arm toward her bag.

"Well, I hope it wasn't the worst," she said dragging the thing over a little. "Sitting with me. You looked like you were on your lunch break."

It'd been a break that long ended shortly after her arrival. I should have clocked back in a while ago and I knew my boss would make me use my sick or vacation time to cover it. That was all right though. I never did stuff like that, so it was all right.

"Not a big deal," I told her wishing I really could express myself more. Sitting with her wasn't a big deal. In fact, it'd been great. "I liked sitting with you."

I had at least gotten that out and her large smile and the light that pushed into her big brown eyes made me grateful I had.

She stood and I did the same. I guess more of that properness my momma taught me.

Getting her bag adjusted, she faced me, tilting her head.

"I enjoyed sitting with you too, Blake," she said, her fingers curling on her bag strap after she got it on. Her grin was full. "In fact, I enjoyed it very much."

Surprised by how that made me feel, I faced away from her, pushing my hands into my pockets to keep from fiddling with them and anything else. She started to roll her bag away and I made a path so she could, the place still busy.

She thanked me with one of her grins and as I needed to head out too, I grabbed my notebook and hat, tossing some extra cash on the table for Maybelle. I had already paid her and tipped her but I figured you could never do too much.

I guess I was taking the example of the girl I had lunch with.

I let her know I wasn't just following her, that I needed to get back to the rock quarry and she merely laughed as I flanked her, telling me that was quite all right.

"If you're looking for a motel there's one yonder," I told her pushing my chin in the direction of the Hen's Inn just down the street. It wouldn't be far for her to walk but with her bag I suddenly wished I had my truck with me. I'd take her but

I left it at the quarry since the diner was within walking distance.

Dang, why didn't I bring that thing?

Lifting my eyes up to the sky, she followed the direction of my gaze, taking a few steps in the direction of the inn. The sign was big enough and I could tell she'd seen it right away, her hand framing her eyes from the high sun.

"I suppose that'll do," she said, placing her hands on the handle of her bag and facing me. "And thank you. That makes things a little easier for me."

"No problem," I said, kicking a little dirt with my dusty boots. "You can rest up real good then. It's a nice place."

I'd never stayed obviously but I'd been to a few parties after some school dances. I also had some buddies that rented rooms out to be with their girls. They bragged on the space and everything.

I hoped those thoughts hadn't materialized on my face and as I'd been known to chase a flush sometimes I scratched the back of my neck.

"Anyway, you should be happy there," I said. "And I hope you have a safe trip when you head back on the road. You here long?"

"Not terribly. Just for the weekend," she told me, spinning around. Her curls caught in the wind. "Long enough where I'll have to find something to do. They got TV and everything? I'm a junky for that." Her face lit up by the prospect and I couldn't help smiling because of it.

"Um, yeah," I said, scratching my neck again. "They got all that for sure."

Her hair fanned on the wind again and in her current, it washed over my face in a way that had me wishing for more time again, more time with her, getting to know her, and seeing what she was about.

I knew, in the end, there really wasn't a point to all that.

She wasn't from here and therefore prolonging anything really wouldn't make sense.

But that didn't stop me from wanting it.

My hand moved out of my pocket as she started to walk away, her pretty brown boots getting caught up with the dust on the actual gravel roads we had here.

"I'm happy I got to meet you," she said. "Eat lunch with you."

She went bashful again, shaking her head.

She lifted it. "But yes, it was fun. I enjoyed it and appreciate you letting me sit."

"It wasn't a problem," I told her, wishing I could emphasize that more. I smiled when I lifted my notebook. "You let me humor you for a little while."

My poke at myself had her eyes doing that hard and soft crinkle again.

"You underestimate yourself, Blake," she said taking a step away again. "Your dreams."

She chewed on her lips and I watched as her steps created more space between us, more distance, and soon that turned into time flashing before my eyes. I saw an hourglass separating the pair of us, the sand almost gone. Only a few granules left, I stepped up to her, watching as she stopped completely and let me get ahead.

"If you're in town for a little while," I said, my jaw moving. "You'll need coffee in the morning?"

Everyone needed that, even a city girl and this Texas boy.

The expression started small, but as I watched that smile spread across her face I knew she'd say yes to my mumbled invitation for coffee in the morning and with her nod, I watched that hourglass fill up just a little. We had more time.

We had more sand.

Three

ANN

ON MY TIPTOES, my hands cupped the window of the diner but I fell back to the soles of my tennis shoes at the sight of an empty building. The sun was terribly high again and I failed to bring one of the many hats packed in my bag.

I didn't want to seem as if I was trying...

Which I was despite myself. Yesterday, Blake had caught me off guard. I'd been sweaty and flushed when I first met him, that sticky train getting to me.

I didn't want to appear that way now, but I had tried, my stretch pants and off-the-shoulder top—pretty but not over the top. It was also a lot cooler than the blouse and boots I wore yesterday and I had no idea if we'd be outside today. The diner was warm and I at least figured my outfit would be good for that.

I popped up on my tennis shoes again, trying to get a peek inside behind the gold lettering on the glass, but the result was just the same. No one was in there on this early Saturday morning, the closed sign up, and that's exactly when Blake said he wanted to meet for coffee.

He may have stood you up.

Though, he hadn't seemed like the type to be that way. He'd been nice, sweet even.

Biting my lip, I couldn't help the reality of my position, though. I was here on a street corner with the front of what was, yesterday, the busiest diner known to man. That diner and street were now empty.

I was here by myself.

Stepping back, my shoes hit the gravel road, my high pink socks keeping the dust from hitting my exposed ankles. Spinning around, I figured the motel television was my next venture until I heard my name.

It took another rotation, to my left and slightly ahead but I saw him clearly, his massive form striking in the harsh light.

Blake seemed different today. He looked different. His faded jeans belted at the waist, he wore a plaid button-up, which seams hit every hard surface of his broad shoulders and overall burly frame. Sitting across from him, I'd been in the wake of his shadow, the man large and no doubt from working. He was in a uniform yesterday, on his lunch break.

He also seemed to bring a peace offering.

The lidded Styrofoam cups in his hand indicated coffee and I grinned, unable to help myself.

I didn't know if it was me or just the fact that I'd noticed him, but his grin rang too though not as full as mine. His lips twitched with it, a splash of red I'd seen before creeping up the side of his neck. With as big as he was he had a bit of shyness to him and reminded me of someone I read in a novel called *Of Mice and Men*, the character Lenny all-encompassing with his size but the insides not so much matching. Blake had that too and he held the cup out toward me, only a few steps between us.

"I thought I'd be here by myself today," I admitted, kind of feeling bad now. Like I said before, he didn't seem like the type to do that.

His head shook every which way as he passed off the coffee, the strong aroma breezing in the already thick wind despite being so early.

"I didn't mean to be late," he said, pushing all that dirty-blond hair out of his face. It looked as if he'd tried to put something in it to keep it back but it had a mind of its own, sitting just past his ears on one side and pushing back behind on the other. The unruly side cut across a set of the palest blue eyes I'd ever seen on someone, enrapturing in a way I had to make sure they were really blue. They looked nearly clear and I properly stared into them for longer than I should have.

Blake hadn't made that easy. His constant gaze aversion possibly stronger than yesterday and him doing that at all hadn't surprised me. A stranger had asked to sit at his table then proceeded to stare at him the whole meal.

"Had to get the coffee," he said raising his arm cloaked in the same blond hair. "Passed by a gas station and picked it up."

Wondering about that, I turned around and faced the diner. His grin had my insides dancing.

"Small town," he told me, stepping over to the diner in his big brown boots. He faced me. "Nothing's open super early on the weekends. Folks are sleeping and everything."

"Folks are sleeping and everything."

I knew I had to have reacted to his accent yesterday, lazy and warm like the thickest, most sweetest honey.

I had to have sounded different to him too and I had no idea yesterday I'd been stopping at all in Texas. The train had malfunctioned and I'd be stuck for nearly two full days, leaving early tomorrow morning.

Maybe that turned out all right in the end.

In that moment, I'd been happy the darkness of my skin didn't visibly flush more than the areas beyond my neck and chest. If so, I'd be fire hot.

Bringing an arm around, Blake guided me. The pair of us

probably looked quite different. I wasn't short or anything, an average five foot five but he had more than a head on me.

He lifted his chin, chiseled-cut and strong.

"I figured we'd take a walk," he drawled, looking at me a little bit before choosing the road in the end. I chose it too. He smiled. "I figured better than TV for a little while?"

His question on the end had me smiling too.

I nodded. This was much, much better than TV.

We circulated the area of the small shops and local businesses, all of them closed but some of them with the owners inside and preparing for the day. Blake got a wave from them, tossing a thick hand and getting a friendly smile each time. Everyone seemed really pleasant here, which was nice.

"Yesterday, um... you said you just graduated?"

I had to read between the lines with him sometimes. He spoke low, deep, and I put on my listening ears to take him in. I found that okay for the most part. It just meant I really had to pay attention, which I didn't mind.

I smiled, nodding after taking a sip of my coffee. "Yeah, I got my bachelor's degree."

His pale blue eyes widened like that was really a feat for him to hear and, perhaps, maybe it was. I often overlooked my opportunities for an education which some didn't have.

Playing with my purse strap across my chest, I tossed my chin at him.

"Did you go to school? College?" I didn't want to assume he hadn't.

His eyes pinched away and I wished I hadn't asked.

"Nah. Never had a reason to. I went to work right after high school."

I wondered when that was, well how much older than me he was. We could have easily been the same age, myself twenty-two.

He didn't dwell on what he said, but hadn't sounded sad

about not wanting to go to college. Perhaps, he wasn't. Maybe school just wasn't something he desired. He had such talent in other ways.

"Did you bring your notebook with you?" I dared to ask him. He looked up and I surprised myself when I bounced on the soles of my shoes a little. "I'd love to see more of them. Your designs I mean?"

His handsome grin filled me up as if *I'd* been asked to show something so special about myself. I could get drunk off the feeling he emitted, a just overall good feeling.

"I figured you might," he said, then stopped in front of a shop window. Tossing his head of dirty blond, he pointed to the window. "How about I show you in there?"

Confused, I came around. I believed most of the shops were closed, but I guess this one wasn't.

I knew because of the large bowl of ice cream sitting in the middle of an empty table.

It sat there, high as a mile and waiting for someone to come inside and do something with it. There were all kinds of ice cream in there, many different kinds of various colors and tones. Awed, I stepped to it and turned to find that flush on Blake's neck again.

Using his finger, he attempted to push some of it away.

"You mentioned ice cream yesterday in the diner," he said and kind of struggling with it like it was hard for him to get out. He shrugged his big shoulders. "I know it's early and we *just* had coffee, but like I said, you mentioned it. It being one of your dreams or something."

He shook his head. Was this really hard for him?

He faced me. "Anyway, you don't have to eat it. It is early and they only had about six flavors so it's not exactly maybe what you wanted?"

He kicked his boot on the sidewalk a little, looking up

when I made it to him so he couldn't stare at the ground anymore.

I made him stare at me, a perfect stranger who'd never had something so sweet and innocent done for her. People didn't do things for me at all, including myself. School had been the one thing I allowed myself to have, the one thing I took as I'd felt strongly about it.

"Will you eat it with me?" I asked, playing with my fingers. I guess I was shy too. "Show me your sketches while we do?"

His lips parted, full and pink and thick.

Kissable, too.

They hiked on the side, slow and hesitant until they made a full smile.

"But you said you wanted to do it by yourself," he said, and I went to tell him that was yesterday, yesterday not today.

Blake actually had his notebook out of sight, on him but not easily seen. I figured he carried it with him always. Like a true artist who had to have their tools ready at a moment's notice in case inspiration was on the horizon, but inside, while we did enjoy that ice cream of many different flavors he expressed to me it wasn't about the sketches. It wasn't about the paper or the prettiness of the designs. It was about the precision and what they'd become off paper. He'd made only a fraction of the designs, the rest ready and waiting for his hands to craft them into reality.

He told me he enjoyed working with wood and something about the intimacy of what he was sharing stirred something within me. He didn't have to tell me these things, his heart exposed to a perfect stranger, but he was.

And we did this all over a bowl of ice cream.

We didn't split the ice cream. We didn't divide it into two separate dishes. We shared it, separate spoons but nothing more divided than that. It was all very intimate, vulnerable for the both of us. By the end, I couldn't finish my measly little dream at all but that had been all right. I had a man the size of two eating with me. Blake cleared what I hadn't and I noticed him slide some money into the shop owner's hand before we left. The amount was well more than six flavors of ice cream should have cost. He also mentioned thanking the owner for opening earlier for us and I figured that was all it was in the end.

The man must have been grateful because he offered me yet another sweet to add to my morning. The shop specialized in cupcakes as well and he opened the case for us, offering one to me on the house.

"You probably didn't expect so much sugar this morning," Blake said as an afterthought. We'd just made it down the street, traveling to seemingly nowhere.

Cradling my cake, I had pride in it. The design was so pretty and almost too good to eat with the pink frosting and silver balls sprinkled on the top. Daring to put it away, I brought my bag around, tucking it deep within the open space.

Shrugging at what he said, I followed him.

"Well, no, but that's okay," I said grinning. "I enjoy sweet things so that worked for me."

I hadn't emphasized what I said or anything but in the back of my mind I knew he'd been a part of that sweet lineup, which one really wouldn't expect from someone like him. Blake could be intimidating at first glance with his size but I think I knew his true secret.

He was nothing but a teddy bear.

Bending over, Blake plucked a piece of straw from a bundle stacked outside the shop, flicking it to the side when he glanced my way. He offered a suggestion of one more stop and I'd been surprised when he led us away from the shops to a nearby water tower. It being a small town, the tower wasn't large at all, maybe a story and he placed his large hands on the ladder.

"My friends and I used to climb up all the time," he said, looking at me. "You can see the whole town."

Reading between the lines, I discerned what he was trying to tell me again. Though, his volume wasn't the issue this time. He'd offered me an invitation, inviting me up.

Completely game, I shifted my bag, wanting to feel like a kid again. Sometimes that was nice, truly.

Blake made sure I had my footing right before I climbed and as the ladder was surrounded by bars like a fire truck I wasn't terribly scared about falling off. Even still, Blake stayed close, covering me and the general area and never letting me get too far ahead.

I knew because I looked down at him often.

The safety features of the water tower remained at the height above, the entire walkway covered in handrails. There was enough space to sit and we did, my knees up while Blake chose to lounge his wide body on his hip, securing a boot to the ledge and gazing out at the drop-off.

It really was a sight to see and I rested my arms on the middle bar dividing the ledge from the handrail.

I'd never been to Texas before and as I'd seen lots of it through the windows of a moving train I realized I truly hadn't seen it.

So much could be taken in at this undistracted height, no trees, only open air and grassy hilltops. Blake's town stretched pretty far beyond the shops and businesses clustered centrally in the center. Lots of land and sectioned-off housing.

"You never said what your degree was for." Hummed in the wind beside me and I realized, in that moment, he'd been watching me, a steady gaze both strong and true.

Soft blue eyes truly did enrapture and I pushed my arms around my legs.

"Medicine, well, nursing," I said not wanting to let on I had the aspirations of a doctor. That job was for someone but had never been what I desired. I smiled. "I enjoyed UCLA's nursing program."

My time there had been some of the most magical experiences of my life, and I would have drawn it out for as long as I could have. I never would have graduated if it had been up to me. I would have just stayed there, a happy forever around me.

But all this might sound odd to someone who didn't know me and I chose to keep the detail to myself, Blake staring on.

"Your dream then?" he asked me, reading me so well despite not knowing me. He grinned a little. "You found mine."

I had and I admitted to defeat to mine as well. Kicking my foot out, I let them both hang off the ledge, falling back to my hands.

"I always liked working with wood," Blake went on, but never had to tell me that. He *showed* me that, his talents on full display in an innocent moleskin notebook. He moved his large bicep over his raised knee.

"Is it like that for you? Nursing?" he asked me.

I nodded again until I realized I had no jurisdiction to. I hadn't actually been given patients beyond school.

"I enjoyed the school bit," I told him. "But all that was then. I'm not seeking employment after school."

This confused him like it probably should, his blond eyebrows drawing together. All these words and not much space between us I knew I'd have to detail things that traveled within the confines of my heart.

But I'd done that same thing to him about his dream...

Smiling, I put on my best face, hoping this stranger couldn't peel it away and see right through me.

"My family is kind of traditional," I told him feeling

rightly silly. This was 1985 for pity's sake.

But try telling my daddy that.

I made my smile stronger. "My dad let me go to school but doesn't want me working."

I had Blake's full attention now, his brow jumping to the height of his blond hairline.

"What would be the alternative?" he asked me, shifting my way completely. The expanse of his broad frame and sudden focus had the rays of a deep vulnerability emanating off me, all of it out there and possibly something he didn't even mean to do.

I swallowed. "I suppose what he and my mama have. Mama doesn't work. Just my daddy. He makes it so she doesn't need to and they both wanted that for me. It was all I could do to convince them to let me go to school."

A master's degree wasn't even an option, not if I actually wanted to be able to come home between terms and see them.

"Just let her go and let her get it out of her system, Daryl."

Mama's words still blasted like a megaphone in my head even still, the greeting I got once I delivered the news of a full ride to UCLA. I worked hard in high school, in the top ten of my class and everything.

The wind blew the heat around, the air getting thick as the sun gained in height. Eventually, it'd be too warm to even be outside.

And then my time with Blake would be done. I'd return to my motel and wait out my train.

I supposed he'd stay here.

My words moved something hard over Blake's expression, something I hadn't recognized, a first between us both. Smoothing it out, he looked at me, dampening his lips a little.

"I guess that sounds silly to me," he said simply. Simple. Like what he'd said was the simplest thing in the word. The lines around his eyes relaxed. "All due respect to your family."

I didn't want to laugh at him in that moment, but really...

He was so dang cute.

My lashes fluttered down. I knew he probably wouldn't like being called that *or* being laughed at.

I ended up gaining control of myself and eventually, pushed my arms around my legs again.

"You're right," I told him because my situation truly was. It was silly for a woman not to work if she wanted to do so. It was all very silly.

I supposed I had always been a silly girl, a foolish girl.

The day truly did start to blaze around us and Blake shifting, I knew he could feel that too. A bit of sweat gathered above his brow and he caught it, lifting a thick hand and even thicker arm.

It was hard not to admire him, the sinews of muscle that formed beneath his arms and shifted on his back. He really did work for a living. He did something incredibly strong.

"I suppose you want to get back to that TV?" he asked after awhile, big puppy dog eyes of blue my way. "I don't want you to melt out here. I know it gets hot."

Something told me it really was my comfort that had him asking and if he hadn't, I knew I would have stayed out there a lot longer before saying something, words close to forever coming to mind.

It was all quite silly these thoughts. As I'd said, I was a silly girl.

He stood before I responded and offered me a hand, one I took willingly and freely. I gathered he did because of our position on the ledge, making it easier for me to get up to him.

I thanked him, not really wanting to let go but easily able to do so. He had marks above his hand, his skin tanned and rough below like they constantly handled things. They worked. They moved with the world around him.

Unable to keep that bright blue gaze again, I started to

walk away toward the ladder that led us up. But like below, his voice stopped me, my name.

He stared at me in a way that made me feel it, made me feel *something* however unusual. But was it unusual?

Was it truly?

He gained on me, looking out toward his little world.

"It isn't the Empire State Building," he said, coming back when he placed a hand on the rail. His gaze lifted. "But it is the highest point in town. No one will hear you if... Well..."

His lips damped as he parted his gaze, choosing to place it out before us.

"I guess I'm just saying it's early. It won't bother nobody. If you want to, that is?"

He found me again but maybe harder the second time around because he didn't get the eye contact, choosing instead to look down at the rail his hand was on.

It took me a second in the open air to figure out what he meant at first, what he wanted me to do. I had to read between those lines again.

And find a language that was his own.

My cheeks hurt with my smile, this man so incredibly sweet. He blinked up at me when I touched his hand and when I gained his eye contact I wouldn't allow him to let go.

I squeezed. "Will you do it with me?" I asked moving into his space. He smelled so nice. Like sunshine in the sky. "I think I wouldn't be brave enough by myself."

He watched me after my words, his throat hiking once before facing out. We both faced his small town and, turning, we let it fly.

I couldn't hear his shout over mine at first, both of us boisterous in the wind as he helped me once again capture my own silly dream. He let me have this one, however tiny, and as I heard his deep voice I became lost in it.

As well as my hand suddenly lost in his.

Four

BLAKE

She wanted me to drive her someplace, her last day and only hours for us. We only had hours, no longer the limitless sand I'd allowed my mind to somehow believe. She'd be gone today. In fact, right after I drove her back to her motel.

I hadn't expected to hear from her this morning, wrapping my head around the fact she'd be gone soon. She told me after we left the water tower yesterday she had a morning train out of town.

But then she called me from her motel phone.

Ann was excited today, her tight coils bouncing in the wind as she pushed a map I had in my glove compartment out on the dashboard of the rickety truck I saved two summers for. She asked for the map the minute she'd gotten in, looking beautiful. I couldn't stop staring at her.

That was the only reason I hadn't fought her.

I should ask her more questions, where we were going and where she was taking me. She'd been super secretive. Like I said, excited. My questions in the wind, I didn't want to waste time on them. Time was the only thing we didn't have.

Instead I watched the road, my knuckles on the wheel as I

made memories, froze in time not what was ahead but beside me.

I memorized her scent and how it combined with the open air coasting through the windows. I memorized how her lashes framed hard around her eyes when she smiled or just talked to me. I memorized her voice, the song in it as she had a tick of a laugh before she spoke sometimes. She did it enough where I knew it came following nerves. I made her nervous.

She made me nervous too.

She made me nervous that I was doing all these things, trying to make memories of something that wasn't mine. We were two people killing time before her train left town today.

I wished that had been all it was. It'd make this whole thing easier and my chest not feel weird every time I looked at her.

"Blake?"

I passed a glance her way, her hard and soft crease of her eyes forming in my direction. One of her plump lips beneath her teeth, she pointed toward what I believed to be the sky, but ended up being a building out in the middle of nowhere.

We were coming up on it, a large factory with big windows and open land around it. I'd never seen it or heard about it, not venturing too far away from where I lived. We'd driven at least fifty miles to get here.

Like I said I didn't question anything she asked me to do.

Via her direction, I turned in the path of the building, a gravel road off the highway.

"Where are we going?" I finally asked her and she simply smiled waving me off and telling me to keep on toward the factory. I might have poked at her more but as the distance between my truck and the factory got smaller I discovered something truly interesting.

Nothing was here, no cars or activity or anything. But I had a feeling that had nothing to do with how early it was or the fact it was Sunday. Enough debris were around where no feet had touched this area for a while and the strategically sized "For Sale" sign ahead could be easily seen from the highway.

I pulled right up to it, turning the truck off after I did. My questions had finally caught up with my brain and I might have presented them to Ann had she not gotten out of my truck so quickly.

Her tennis shoes on the ground, she scampered off, wrapping the tiny strap of her bag around herself before closing the creaky truck door with her hip. She waited for me as I came around, her smile bright in the wind.

"What is all this?" I asked, amazed by her. She navigated us here like this area was her roots and not mine.

I had a feeling that had something to do with the flyer in her hand, the one I caught her looking at a couple times. Fisting it, she opened it up, comparing the image on it to the one before us, an abandoned building of some sort. On the front labeled: Princeville Shoe Company.

Apparently satisfied, she came back to me, lowering her flyer. For the first time in our journey, I caught a glimpse of that vulnerability I sometimes saw in her, the meekness back and on display in front of me. It caused the flush to creep along her chest and her delicate neck.

Her curls breezing in the wind, she came to me, making my vulnerability show most assuredly.

"There was a posting for this place on the community board at the motel this morning," she said facing it before facing me. "I want to show you something. Do you have your notebook?"

Always having it, I pulled it out of my back pocket, the thing tiny enough to fit in there. Trusting her with it, I gave it to her, realizing I'd never done that. I'd never given it to anyone before.

She received it like it was the most precious treasure, opening to a page before asking me to follow her.

I wasn't sure about all that, this place not ours to roam or anything but as it seemed abandoned I ventured the yard with her. The place was gated but we'd already driven through that part, the gates broken and rusted, open. This shoe factory hadn't been in production for a long time.

I kept my strides short not to get ahead of her, her little hips wiggling their way to the far-wide door. Her jeans hugging her frame and her top off her shoulder, I watched, keeping my distance as much as I could. I wasn't getting too close to her.

I'd *already* gotten too close to her.

She made it to the old factory door first, opening the steel latch with her free hand. Upon turning the knob, it opened right away for her and I eyed her, stepping forward in my boots.

"Did you know that'd open?" I asked her and she simply grinned.

"I hoped it would."

She said that with a smile that made her eyes widen, asking me to follow her with a jerk of her head. She took the first steps forward but as I had no idea what we'd be getting into with this place, I reached ahead and held the door, my arm out and covering her as we cut through the dust of the old factory.

The air was thick with age, musty and other smells that told of time. They hadn't been bad smells, fine leather amongst them. That was exactly what we'd found, shoes every-where amongst overturned chairs and tables. There was steel equipment and their accompanying conveyer belts, truck lifts and some of them still holding the pallets or boxes they'd been in the process of lifting away. The place also had a second level that led to an unknown destination, but it was all fascinating, making me feel as if I was getting a peek of something I wasn't supposed to.

The whole thing excited Ann. Her eyes lit up as she spun around freely.

"It's even better than I thought," I heard her say but didn't focus on the comment long.

I watched her hand, disappearing in mine when she reached out. We'd done that yesterday too and I'd hated when I ultimately had to let go.

I hated this moment too, knowing I'd have to let go again.

Forming my fingers around hers, I studied her softness, my hardened palms the looking glass. She was soft, so perfect and she squeezed my hand too, coming forward.

"I'm going to take the risk in overstepping," she said looking up at me. She dampened her lips. "But I feel it's important. Can I?"

I had no idea what she was asking me and she had to know that, but even though she hadn't asked specifics I figured out on my own what I thought she really wanted from me.

And that was to trust her.

I did, though I didn't know her. It was all something I didn't understand and I bet she didn't either. It was all so confusing, her, *me and her*.

Nodding, I allowed my boots to move as she guided us into the center of the factory's operation. She still had my notebook in hand and she turned to a page quickly with her thumb. Grinning, she stared up at the rafters of the shop, spinning until we came across one of the largest abandoned machines.

Letting go there, she cradled my notebook, staring up at me.

"This is your production line," she spoke out into the air, the sun cascading light across her high cheeks. A direct ray shown down from the skylight above, shining on the dust in the room and making it look like glitter or something across the room.

She brought the notebook over to the assembly line and I followed her, the book open on a tiny children's toy I'd yet to make. It was designed to be made out of wood. They all were.

She put her hand over the drawing, again like it was precious or something, then gestured toward the conveyer belt behind her.

"It'll be self automated," she said nodding with a smile. She faced the conveyer belt. "Your men will make everything right with a push of a button."

"My men?"

The question was both internal and external, not under-standing what she was saying. But Ann... she didn't give me a moment to catch up.

Sprinting with my notebook, I was hard pressed to catch her, her tennis shoes taking her clear over to the other side of the room. There were tables here, all holding shoes, letter scraps and whatnot. Here was where Ann turned more pages, and by the time I noticed where she stopped, she was already speaking again.

"But these are so precious," she said, eyeing me when I noticed the music box under her hand pressed to the pages of the book. Sliding off, she touched a table full of shoes, looking up and into the light.

She closed her eyes like she was trying to feel something, channeling something.

She opened them.

"Your people will make the things by hand here," she spoke on, lifting her hand. "You'll have so many employees. People dying to work for Blake and bring his sketches to life."

I was afraid to take in air, make a sound as my boots scraped the way and went her direction.

She let me, the small world tiny between us. I was trying to get what she was saying, where she was going with this and why.

My hand went out and she took it again, cutting off anything and everything I might have said. Instead, she pulled me, took me to places I wasn't sure I was capable of seeing. It seemed too farfetched.

It seemed not meant for me.

Even still, this city girl took me there, stopping in front of an area completely empty. There were no distractions there, no old boxes, crates of shoes or tools. There was just us, us and the air and the world.

"But you'll keep your rocking chairs here," she said, staring out like she could see them and when I came behind her, she already had the page found.

One of my rockers was right under her thumb, not one that I wanted to make, but one I'd made time and time again for people in my town. I got to see the things everywhere, everyone wanting one when they saw someone else's. Since the first one I made, they never stopped and the joy I got from seeing them...

Ann's breath hiked when I came behind her, her eyes closing when she opened them out to the empty area.

"They're so special, Blake," she said nodding. "They're special and they'll be here, ready and waiting for each order. You'll ship them around the world one day. Everyone will want your rocking chairs."

The world...

She left me but only just, choosing to go toward the closest wall. My book closed, she let it fall to her hip, staring up yonder and above at that secret world we couldn't see from the first level.

I went to her, again staying with her. I looked on with this girl, trying to see what she had already said. I couldn't see the assembly line or even the employees, but I had to see whatever this was.

The visions in her head had her smiling, her head lowering with them.

"Up there, the king of the castle will be of course," she told me tipping her chin in the direction of the second level. "There's where your office will be, a place for you to escape it all sometimes. A place where you can just catch your breath."

"And where will you be?"

I spoke behind her, always behind her and I watched her shudder as I placed a hand on her hip and took her in. I indulged in the things both my heart and mind wanted, the feel of her waist as hips turned to thigh, the smell of her hair when she tilted her head.

Her eyes closed, letting me breathe her in, letting me absorb her and, slowly, her hands went ahead not touching mine but to the wall.

"Here," she said, her dark lids sliding over her eyes. Opening them completely, she turned around, leaving my hands enough to touch me, her hand on my face and in my hair.

I felt every degree of heat, the charged electrodes circulating down to my boots. Stepping forward, she pushed her fingers in, her sweet smell so close I could taste it on my tongue.

"And here," she said, her fingers so embedded in my hair she was nearly inside me. She was inside, but she was wrong about something.

Proving that to her, I took her hand and moved it to my chest, the beats I was sure she could feel straight through my shirt.

"Here," I told her. "*Here*, you'll be."

Her hand slid easy when I removed it from my chest and

she came in even easier when I pushed my hand behind her neck.

My lips slammed down on hers without resolve, a constant and fervent reverie between that of our lips.

I hugged her to me by her hips, feeling her body literally giving way and submitting to me. It gave out, her hands clenched to my chest as she let herself fall.

Her taste challenged all senses, opened them up and let them ring to their full potential. Colors were brighter, tastes were warmer and richer.

Touch was stronger.

My hand gripping the back of her neck, I edged her mouth open with my tongue, watching that give way too, watching her let me open her up. I worked my way in, tasting and dancing along this high with her. I let myself meld into the dream with her.

I let her take me there.

Five

ANN

IT TOOK a lot to get Blake to come to my motel room with me. He wasn't that kind of guy and I knew that right away, probably within moments of meeting him.

But I wasn't that girl either. I didn't *do* this with someone I just met. That had been the point. Neither one of us did this.

But we were doing it anyway.

Once he was there, he hadn't resisted. He no longer resisted... this, letting me unbutton his shirt and touch him in all the ways I wanted to touch him. I wanted to see his body. I wanted to *feel* the muscles shift and move beneath my hands while he thrust his heat inside me. I wanted him in all the ways a woman wanted a man, unashamed and passionate.

My hands pushing over his shoulders slid his shirt down his biceps, his arms coming around my hips as we sat on my bed. He brought me off my knees and to him, his body a massive force of hardened planes and steel biceps.

He used the thickness of his hands to undress me, pushing my top off my shoulders until they were as bare as his.

His lips parted on the top of one, my eyes closing as he pushed a hand beneath the shirt. He unclasped my bra this way, a maneuver that told me he'd not only done this before but well. Placing me on my back, he let the bra give way, pressing himself on me and chasing soft kisses on my lips.

His weight on me, I couldn't breathe. I didn't want to, afraid of what would happen when I did. Thinking was a bad idea, thinking might end this and push him away.

Incredibly warm, he caged me, pulling off my shirt and then sliding my bra to the side. He pushed his thumbs along the inside of my arms, breathing warmth against my nipples too hard and achy below him.

His tongue tasted before it laved, exploring fingers pinching and tweaking my dark areolas.

"Blake..."

My legs parted to let him in, the feat apparent with his size. My ankles couldn't even lock around his waist, my calves aiding my hips to rise and fall with the grind I attempted to make against his jeans.

Each roll of my hips, I felt him harden, considerable steel between my legs. Using a hand, he helped me out, gravity keeping his heat away from me.

He moved my hips with me, his thrusts slow in return. Pushing his hand down my thigh, he gripped my bottom.

"Tell me this is a bad idea," he whispered, pressing a kiss to my breast before tasting. He nipped with his teeth, blond hair cascading around him. "Tell me you're not meant for me."

I could tell him all these things. I *knew* all these things, but despite that I couldn't turn him away.

Maybe because somewhere in my heart I longed for another truth, another reality in which we ended up together. It felt so real I actually believed it. I was his.

We'd always end up this way every time.

It didn't matter the probability or that alternate reality. Somewhere we were together. Somewhere we were each other's.

I stopped him but only to look at him, lifting my head to part my mouth on his chin.

"It's not true, Blake," I said. "None of it's true."

What he said was false. This was our reality.

This was our truth.

His mouth moved into mine when I guided it that way, unclasping my jeans and pushing his fingers into them. He peeled them away with my panties, my arousal in the air and his full fingers ready to explore it.

His hand between my legs peeked at heaven, his mouth just as sweet. His thick fingers tunneled their way inside me, his thumb drumming over my tender bud. He nearly made me come that way, with his hands.

"I want you inside," I told him, using my calves to once again draw him to me. "I want you here."

Sliding his fingers out, I made him cup me, my warm juices between us. Watching him, my hips moved, his eyes closing as I slid away and unbuckled his jeans.

My legs falling away, I pushed the denim and his underwear down his tree trunk thighs, greedy and incredibly needy as I watched him kick them off and expose himself to me.

He arched full up to a ripped torso, my imagination not nearly as accurate as the real display. The build of a man towered over me, his member thick and a smattering of blond hairs around it. Blake massaged himself, forcing precum to seep from the tip.

He took my mouth as he locked me down with his weight again, his hand doing a dance with his jeans when he gathered protection for us from his wallet. Once he got it on he no longer restricted himself. He covered me, pushing himself between my legs and pressing me down hard to the bed.

"Ann..."

He breathed my name just as he slid the head in, his considerable size stopping and waiting for my body to adjust.

His hand behind my neck, he eased my mouth open with soft kisses, taking my mind to other places while he guided in inch by considerable inch.

He was so thick and full. My thighs parted, hitting the bed while he pushed himself, pushed me. Once inside, he stopped, looking at me.

He watched with each thrust, each moment slow and calculated like he was making sure this was okay, that *I* was okay. With my return, he picked up movement, his thighs humming a warmth before slamming a burn between my legs.

I knew I called for him. I called for God and everything else I could think of, my head rolling back, as I felt things I never felt before. It was different when it was someone I felt a true connection with.

It was wonderfully different.

Blake had his eyes closed, complete and pure ecstasy on his face with each move of his thick hips. Picking up, the legs of the bed moved, scraping across the carpet and the steel bed frame hitting the back of the wall. At one point, he actually apologized. I kissed him and guided him not to stop. I didn't care what we did to the room.

I just cared what he did to me.

Once he wasn't self-conscious about it, he continued his movements, reaching back to gain more control of the bed. With his strength, he managed to do it, picking up my hips with the movement of his. I felt the minute he was close, his thrusts piston-like, constant and strong. Arched, he spilled into me the same moment warmth flurried inside my tummy.

The room spun, my body locked and unable to come down from the high. It took Blake's hands cupping the back of my thighs to realize I'd finally relaxed from release, his arms waiting to catch me.

Of course he was there to catch me.

Six

BLAKE

I MUST HAVE FALLEN ASLEEP, the hour still early. I reached for Ann but she wasn't where I left her. She'd been on me, so close we'd been one person nearly.

Disoriented, confused, I turned on my side, trying to gather my wits and figure out exactly what I was doing. My mind felt caught in a turbine.

My heart even worse.

Scrubbing my hands down my face, I took a much-needed breath, then pushed myself from beneath the sheets. I wanted to find Ann, talk to her.

I wanted to figure out whatever this was.

My insides were telling me one thing but my brain another. My head was the logical one, the guy saying all the things my insides didn't want to hear. He was talking them down, telling them to come down from all this and get back to reality.

But sometimes the brain wasn't always the right thing to trust.

We were in an age of phones and travel. If we wanted to stay connected... stay *something* to each other, we could. It was possible. It wasn't that farfetched. Both of us were scared to shit of planes but we could try and make something happen if it was worth it.

We'd just have to try a little bit.

And if something worked out, truly worked out I'd be willing to uproot.

I wondered if she had the same considerations. I wondered if she was considering them now, sitting off to herself and contemplating like I was. This all was a lot and if we had time, we *both* needed to breathe. We were both rightly interworked with each other right now, too close to make any logical decisions.

But like I said, we didn't have time.

I didn't bother with my clothes, getting out of bed. A quick exit wasn't what this was, a careless moment in the wind that now I was trying to get out of it. That wasn't the type of guy I was, never had been. I wanted to talk to Ann and figure all this out.

I ended up getting out the left side of the bed, the one closest to the motel phone, and I took notice of the phone for a strange reason.

The phone was gone but the cord still there, outstretched and leading away as if the whole phone was taken. Following it, I came across the bathroom I barely noticed when we got in the room. The door had been open then.

It wasn't now.

A light shone underneath it, a person inside and the cord leading right underneath. She'd taken the whole phone in the bathroom and was on it. Normally, I would have given her privacy and I almost did before something told me to stop, listen.

The logical one in this had my hand touching the door, her voice behind it and talking to someone else. That someone else had her whispering quietly, mentioning words of, "don't worry," and words of, "I'll be home soon."

At first I believed she might have been talking to her parents or even a friend or another family member, but as I listened on, her voice sweet and her tone low...

Her words spoke of comfort, soothing and purely intimate. The nature went beyond a parent or even a close friend and when she spoke a male's name, another, "Don't worry," in her voice the son of a bitch inside my head told me the harsh truth. He brought me down and told me exactly what this was.

However cruel.

I honestly couldn't tell you the guy's name she said if asked. I forgot about it the moment I heard it, but once I had I nodded, coming away from the door. The creak in the flooring under the carpet was audible and I assumed she heard me the moment I made it. It'd been loud enough but I didn't care. She should know I overheard her.

I shouldn't have been listening anyway.

Back to the bed, I shrugged on my boxers and pants and the far wall casted light when the bathroom door open. The light flickering off, I proceeded to look down and find the rest of my clothes. Ann had made her way back out by then and I felt her before I saw her.

Her scent squeezed me tight, her floral aroma chasing its way into my chest and messing up my insides like it had that first hour, the first moment of her known existence to me.

I saw her bare feet when she stood in front of me. I'd been putting on my socks and shoes.

She said nothing as I got them on, her smooth legs leading up to panties covered by nothing but the top she'd worn today. I only knew because her legs and waist were in my direct line of sight. I didn't look up at her. No phone cord was by her legs and I assumed she'd returned the phone to the end table.

"Blake?"

My fingers went to my shirt, buttoning it up. I would have managed just fine.

But then she had to go and intercede.

Taking over the buttoning for me, she sat to my side on the bed.

She kept her head down, her head a wash of those spiral curls. I could taste their smell again, Ann too close.

I got to study every line of her face from the harsh dip of her cheekbones to the smooth curves of her lips. Her framed eyelashes in the direction of my buttons kept her attention away from me, my greedy observations of her.

And they had been greedy. She truly wasn't mine.

Upon finishing, her fingers stopped at the button pressed warmly to my chest, her hand flattening the hem out before falling away.

We sat there, beside each other. Many questions but also undeserved answers between us. Eventually, I had to ask her. I couldn't assume.

"Who is he?" I asked eventually, not looking at her.

The words came out harsher than I wanted them to and with more disdain and emotion than I had the right to. I had no right to her. Like I said...

She wasn't mine.

Ann's legs crossed in my direction, her smoky brown legs brushing my jeans.

"Someone from home," she settled on. "A guy from home."

This could mean anything and I was sure that's why she said it that way.

I breathed. "Are you with him then or..." I pushed my hands down my face, again not looking at her. "Are you with somebody, Anita?"

I wasn't the type of person to be with someone if they

were already involved. I wouldn't take a woman from another man out of respect and dignity. That was just the type of person I was and how I'd been taught.

But Ann wasn't from here, was she?

My head talked to me again, saying things of foolishness and kicking me hard, my brain saying it didn't rightly give a damn about me or my heart.

Ann's hand came down on my arm and as much as I hated it, I let it stay.

Because I knew I'd hate it falling away even more.

"We're not together, Blake," she said, relieving the pace of my heart only a little. She had something in her voice that told me she wasn't finished, a breath there like there were more words.

Her hand squeezed on me before it pushed and when she touched her forehead down on my shoulder I closed my eyes.

"But we're expected to be... in the end," she continued, cutting away, and that dagger deepened. I truly couldn't breathe.

And I hated my lungs for it.

Ann went on to tell me things I didn't want to hear, speaking about tradition and all the things that meant something where she came from versus where I came up. She wasn't with this guy now but she had been in the past, something they cut off right before college. They wanted to live, be with others and experience life. The intention was to come back to each other, a pairing that wasn't an official betrothal but basically put together by her parents. They both came from affluent families. They knew in the end that's what this would be, but what I didn't know, what she hadn't told me was one more thing that involved her and us, a nothing that hadn't even existed forty-eight hours ago. It hadn't been two full days since we met, merely a few hours more than twenty-four. We really meant nothing.

Especially when you compared it to a lifetime of something and someone.

Her arms had pushed around mine at this point, her cheek on my shoulder so warm it could burn me through my shirt. It was burning me, a brand I didn't want or desire. I didn't wake up that morning for work the day I met her expecting anything like this. I didn't ask for it.

My lids fell hard on my eyes, behind them burning like inside my chest. Eventually, I couldn't deal with them anymore. It was just too much.

I touched her hand on my arm, but that's all I could do.

"We should get you to the train station," I said, knowing it was time for that. "I can drive you. I can take you there."

Seven

ANN

I THOUGHT about all the things I should have said, all the things that *should* have been said.

My vision panned to the side mirror, Blake's large and encompassing frame outside of his old Ford pickup. He pumped gas, his vision away from me as it'd been since we left the motel. He offered to drive me though I could have walked.

I should have walked.

My arms moved around me, my head down. There were so many things I should have said. I should have told him I was standing up for myself. I should have told him I was going to change things. I wouldn't do the things expected of me.

I'd choose a different path.

I looked toward him again but he ventured from the truck at this point. I watched as his large back moved in the direction of the gas station, his intent I assumed to pay for the gas he'd just pumped. He'd come out and that would be it.

We'd be strangers again.

The wait forced a hurt inside me that wasn't justified. In a way, at least how we were leaving things, had been my fault. I would have liked to say we never should have slept together, that I never should have met him the day after we met for coffee, or that I should have sat with him for lunch in the first place. I'd like to say all those things, but they'd be lies. I'd been lying to myself. Meeting him had actually allowed me to have more beyond the best day, making me feel like I had when I treated patients. I felt the same purpose of when I did the job I never got to have.

How fitting as I never got to have him either.

His silhouette could be seen through the gas station window, Blake in line as he waited to pay. In that moment, watching him must have been too much for me because I panned away, trying to look at anything and feel nothing. In that fruitless journey, I studied his seat, the moleskin notebook sliding into my hand when I reached for it. He always had it on him, but apparently not this moment.

My hand smoothed over the nearly flawless yet worn cover, feeling even more of those feelings I didn't want to feel. They hurt so much.

I opened my eyes, not knowing they were closed and I panned to the right again, studying Blake's large frame. He'd gotten up to the attendant and I used that time to reach into my purse. Finding a pen, I opened his notebook. If I couldn't say the things that needed to be said...

I could at least write them down.

Eight

BLAKE

WE SAT in the cab of my truck, even breaths too loud in there. Neither one of us moved. Though, I think we both knew she should have left a while ago. Her train was here, loading.

I could hear it.

We sat in the parking lot, waiting while time passed us by, waiting for what I didn't know but Ann must have figured it out.

I felt her before she actually touched me again. Her smell so soft in the wind. She got so close but I didn't turn. If I had our lips would have met.

I just couldn't... do that. It'd be too much and sending me down a rabbit hole I didn't know if I could work my way out of again. I knew she wasn't meant for me now.

No sense in giving false hope.

I waited for what she'd do, what she'd say but I ended up being wrong in the second account. She chose to *do* something and that was put her hand on my bicep.

As well as kiss my cheek.

Inside me and everywhere, I felt this city girl's lips. She

could get that deep with me and, perhaps, for the rest of my life if I ever saw her again. I had not much hope of that. She lived too far away.

She lingered after her lips left mine, her forehead touching my temple once before her hand slid away from my arm, the absence of which I felt immediately. She was falling away from me, disappearing with every moment and every ounce of breath that passed.

Say something to her...

My lips couldn't say the words, my damn brain, my damn bastard brain. He wouldn't say anything, putting a vise on my heart. Stuck in the vault of silence, I watched someone I had a connection with grab her purse from the floor of my truck and push it over her shoulder. The crack of the door came next, her duffle she had with her up front hitting the ground. I assumed I'd hear her footfalls in the wind but from her side came something I thought I had on me.

The moleskin notebook slid into the dip of her seat it was so smooth, and for the first time, I chose to directly look into Ann's line of sight.

I captured her fully with my gaze, drank her in from the curls whipping around her in the wind to her large dark eyes that thirsted themselves on me as well. We feasted, both selfish and without hope. Because there wasn't any.

This was our reality.

Ann's lips moved and I hoped *she'd* be the one to say something. She could get my brain's rear in gear, make him get out of my way to be the man I knew I was and do something. I could tell a girl I had a good time with her. I could tell her I liked her...

So many damn things.

But neither of us said anything. I guess both of us were weak in the end. Smiling at me, Ann at least let me have that, her fingers lifting before closing the door. Her head dipping, she severed her gaze and I couldn't even watch as she lifted the handle of her bag and dragged it away. I couldn't watch her walk away. Instead, I chose to grab the notebook, something falling out of it.

A slip of paper slid across the same seat my notebook had been on, the paper the same as in the notebook itself. It'd been ripped out and when I turned it, it had writing on the page.

A list was there, a short list but a list. It had things like "eat an entire bowl of ice cream with many different flavors," and "shout from the highest point in town." Both things had been checked off and at the bottom the final thing with yet a similar check beside it.

Have the best day(s).

She'd put the "s" like that, the word "days" underlined. She checked it like she accomplished it, like she accomplished everything on her list.

Bones crushed inside my chest as if in a collision, my insides hollow and the fervent emptiness making it hard to breathe. I couldn't even hold the paper she'd written, the scrap falling from my fingers. I ended up opening the notebook for some reason, the spine broken to the page she ripped out and there I saw more writing.

There I saw all I needed to see.

My boots moved in the wind and I didn't even go inside the train station, knowing she'd already be inside. Her train was already loading. She would have rushed to be let on.

I went to the track, looking through the windows with my notebook and I passed the window she sat in front of at first. I had to go back, but I knew it was her.

Her curls were in the wind, her head against the window frame.

"Anita!"

Half the people on the platform looked at me, Ann amongst them.

She turned as if startled, rising up and immediately.

I held up the notebook, her words in the air between us.

They said, "Never forget your dreams," and "Always remember them, Blake."

"If you will," I started, moving forward. I shook the notebook at her. "I will."

She knew what I meant. She had to. She may have been going home and into some universe to be with this guy.

But she could still live her dream.

Her mouth opening, I watched her eyes. All that empty space lifted the moment her eyes did that thing I loved, that soft and hard crinkle thing.

They lit her large eyes up, a sheen in them I could see from the platform.

She put her hand to her chest, nodding.

"I promise, Blake," she said, her voice thick and cast with emotion. She nodded again, a tear falling into her lap. "I promise."

I nodded too and so tall, I knew I could get to her from where I stood.

I reached up, right into the train for her hand.

"Be safe," I told her wishing I'd said something else. I wanted to tell her to be happy and that I'd always remember her.

Gripping my hand, she held it as if a lifeline. I did too. It was a lifeline.

She nodded again, pushing her hand over her eyes.

We stood that way for a while, for as long as the train conductor would let us. Eventually, I had to let go and even after I did, I watched. I watched until the train moved out of my sight.

I *made* the short-term moment, the longest of memories.

Nine

BLAKE

St. Albert's Hospital
El Paso, Texas
Four years ago... continued.

IT'D BEEN like waking up, like being inside heaven with just as much light around me. It shined through my hospital room —on her and being unable to see her was impossible. I refused to lose her.

A ghost of a dream.

Her response to her name had been little more than a head raise in the sunshine, her hair up big and busy, but even with those curls fastened up real tight I still remembered how they played in the light. How each and every ray reflected off the pretty brown tone and made the strands of her hair more hazel than dark brown, the same with her eyes...

Her eyes that held age lines now, more than thirty years into the future but that the only sign of time passed, the curve of her full pink lips plush and her cheekbones as high. Her features were just as soft as the last hours I'd seen them.

Soft...

My fingers bunched at my side over my hospital sheet, still… feeling her in those last moments, her deep brown skin flushed everywhere, her body heated.

I'd been heated too, impulsive and I wondered if that had to do with why some of it had played out the way it had. I wondered for a long time if I'd scared her off. If *I* had been the reason she left in the end and not fate and life in general. The thoughts had been anything I could do to rationalize the situation, that it *had to have been* me.

That I just hadn't held on tight enough.

Her movement toward me in her hospital scrubs came as something of an aberration. She couldn't be here. Not after all this time and so close. I lived not far from this hospital. She couldn't be here.

Ann…

But she responded to me when I said her name. She *came* to me and this time she stayed, her hand bunching just as much at her side like she didn't know what to do. I'd had a *heart attack*, been in and out for days and was just as unclear about this situation as my time under. I was out of it. She wasn't here.

But then…

Pink flowers, *peonies* in the wind when the gorgeous and fluid woman lifted her hand to her head, catching one of those curls I knew was still just as big and vibrant as the last time I'd seen them out. I only wished I could see her dance, wish I could see those curls flowing big and wide.

The actual thought of all that time missed, passed emotion in me, all those dances I was sure she had in her life I hadn't gotten to see. Because I hadn't been strong enough to keep her, hold on and tell her what I should have those last moments, how things could have been all right with us and despite us being strangers she didn't have to go. She could have *stayed* with me, but as I watched her watching me I decided to let it all go. I had to. Because she had left she'd been able to live her own life and I mine, my boys, the families and lives they were starting to build the greatest product. I wouldn't give any of that up for nothing.

But I wouldn't give up the chance to see her again either.

Ann's hand fell from her face. "Blake, I…"

Her fingers found their way in mine when I grabbed her hand. She'd probably been about to say something significant but I couldn't help stopping her. I saw her hand start to retreat, go away, so I grabbed it.

I had to have her hand in mine.

I didn't think about her life, who she was now and where she was going. I honestly didn't even really put together her purpose in this hospital besides being a nurse and put no ties really to what I was doing. I just wanted to hold her, whatever that meant, feel her if not one more time.

And she let me.

Her lips parting, she let me, so much emotion playing on her face. It placed shine in her brown eyes and made them just as big, as wide as they'd been that day, those hours that placed a lifetime in both my heart and mind.

"Where have you been?" I asked her, not why was she here or even who she was now. I just wanted this question answered.

I didn't think I could have chosen it if I wanted to.

Ann

We talked for hours. We could have talked for days if his family would have allowed him to. They checked on him often, his beautiful family of strong men who looked just like him. They passed me little more than a glance, but with the flashes of the light blue eyes of their father more respect and upbringing in their acknowledgement than most men twice their age. Blake had instilled so much good in them, their hearts I knew had to be just as big. I gave them their time with him, their families and girlfriends, as well as the rest of Blake's kin, but with each interruption, I knew in my heart I couldn't leave the room. Blake would always see me, never letting go despite his family's attention. He'd keep his gaze on me, leaving from them just long enough to let me know he was still here, that he wanted *me* there.

Just like his handhold.

His touch had been just as magnetic as it had all those years ago, and though I hadn't known what it meant, I let him. I still let him. Every time his family moved away and left us alone it was just autopilot. Like we *had* to do that, regardless of our stories and backgrounds. I hadn't seen a spouse on his chart and with the various conversations of his family I found out he wasn't married or tied to anyone. He hadn't asked about my current involvements either in our short time together, but I honestly didn't believe that was what our hand-holds were about. We were reconnecting.

We were finding each other again.

"You saved me," he said at one point in our conversation, after how I told him how I'd come to work at this hospital. My journey had simply taken me there, something in the back of my mind strong after the divorce I had from my previous husband.

I think for a long time I knew the decision wasn't right even back then to go to him and my home, but it took going through that situation for me to learn what it truly felt like to have something special that meant something. I needed to live my own life, be my own person, and I ended up coming to work in the only place I had ever felt that. Blake got me to see so much in such a short amount of time. He'd never truly left me and it seemed I hadn't left him either.

Laughing, I felt the rough grooves in his hand. This man worked for a living, always so big and strong.

"I think the doctors had something to do with that," I told him, responding to his previous statement, but I helped. I battled with him. "And your strong heart."

He'd been the true warrior, his body physically unable to quit and with his wonderful family I knew why. He had so much to live for.

Blake's thick fingers played in my palm, like he was holding on to whatever moments he had before his family returned, capturing them. Bringing my hand in, he brought me close. He did something that pulsed pricks of liquid to my eye ducts again.

He placed my hand on his chest, his big broad chest, which was just as hard and muscular as it'd been that day at the factory, the day I showed him what I always saw inside of him, the depth of the dream so visceral I'd had to share.

The beats inside this man remained the same, so strong like that big heart I told him about.

"You saved me," he whispered again, and I saw something in *his* eyes now. Emotion in a man I didn't believe particularly shared his feelings too often. There had been so many tears when his family came in to visit him, even knowing he was okay and would pull through. They shared that emotion for him anyway.

He shared it for me now.

Squeezing my hand on his chest, he looked at me, his heat buried deep within my palm. He reached up, touching my eyes when my tears finally fell. I couldn't help them anymore.

I finally felt at home.

"You saved me too," I said, cupping his hand to my cheek, and even though I knew nothing, didn't know where we were going or what we were doing from here, I did something just as impulsive as that day.

I leaned forward and kissed him. His mouth so hot and wonderful I knew this dream to actually be true. Especially when he slid his hand over the back of my head and kissed me with just as much power as he had all those years ago. It'd been during that time he changed my life.

It'd been the beginning of our wonderful start.

Ten

COLTON (BLAKE'S YOUNGEST SON)

Today

POP HAD TOLD me about how he and my stepmom met, told us all about the kind woman who had taken care of him after he had his heart attack four years ago. We'd all believed Ann to have just been his nurse at the time, as he'd left out their entire history, the head of our family always so private. My brothers and I never found out the truth of their intricate past until the day our pop and Ann got married. The two revealed everything during their wedding vows at the small chapel not even a year after his heart attack. The two of them spoke about a chance meeting, two people by fate finding something neither of them had been expecting. It'd been so powerful the connection had stayed with them long after they parted ways, choosing other lives and a path they both believed had been destiny.

I guess they couldn't have been more wrong because *destiny* had actually been choosing themselves in the end.

They'd been battling an ultimate end, which they both ended up finding out after they came back into each other's lives four children and two marriages later from that first day. Ann never ended up staying with her husband and my pop, well, things with my mother didn't work out. Our parents' fallout had been well before I had memories of it, but from how my brothers made it sound, my pop moving on from Momma had been the best thing for him and as it seemed, he got the best of both worlds. My brothers and I existed because of our mother.

And in the end he got to have his dream anyway.

His dream came in the form of Ann and the wonderful business she had been involved in building up, the history of *Chandler & Sons*, Pop's furniture company, another surprise to us all. We'd all worked in some form for our pop, my oldest brother, Hayden, the business manager, my older brother Brody a driver, and Griffin both a financial benefactor as well as being involved in the general business dealings. Pop designed the furniture and I'd given him my own artwork for the business branding from time to time, something I dabbled in. None of my brothers knew we ended up playing a part in the creation of the very place where a woman showed a man his potential destiny. The very factory Ann showed him, Pop ultimately purchased, that old shoe factory out in the middle of nowhere. He may have bought it after his heart attack four years ago, but he'd been working toward a down payment for the place well before his heart gave out.

He'd been working toward it well before his soul mate came back into his life.

I saw it all the time, how he felt about her, how she opened him up and made him alive in a way I'd never seen. She'd done something to him, well before us and with her history, she told us the same about him.

Ann explained she came back to Texas to continue living

her dream of nursing, but it was only after our pop became her patient did she realize she'd really ended up there for him, hoping, praying one day their paths would cross again in that same town, the hospital she chose only a town away from where my pop grew up. She had coffee in the diner they met in every morning before work, something she told us outside of Pop's ears.

Hearing all of this put something in perspective for me, something I'd been privy to watching my brothers create their own relationships and families over the years but never truly resonating until I heard my pop and Ann's story. It showed me right there, true evidence of what life could truly be like, the power of it and as it turned out, I'd only gotten a sample from my brothers and their various relationships. The true romancer, as it turned out, was the head of our family, our pop, a man once so closed off and gruff I never once thought sharing his life with another was even on his radar, but I'd been so wrong. The love he had for Ann changed him and brought the light out of him that allowed him to be his true self. He finally got to be who he always should have been and love made that possible.

Nothing but love.

EMPIRE STATE BUILDING
NEW YORK CITY, NEW YORK

Today

Epilogue

ANN

TIME COULD BE AN UNUSUAL THING. It could be tragic. It could be sad but also oh so special. It could turn a young woman whose only value for herself came from pleasing others and shift her into one who took ownership of her own destiny. It could help her find her own dreams and not only discover them but *live* them. I caught a glimpse into my destiny during a short trip, back in 1985. I'd spent all day on a train and wanted nothing more than for that train to never stop. I wanted it to take me far away and nowhere near my home-town of New York City. I knew fate awaited me there and a life I wanted nothing to do with since I discovered that's where I'd be headed. How ironic that when that train did stop...

I never wanted it to keep on.

I saw my life during that short stop, what I was supposed to be and who I was supposed to be that person with. I think Blake had seen it too, but he'd been scared. He'd been scared to take ownership of it like me.

We were no longer scared.

I smelled him in the wind. I felt him around me when so

many others ventured along the same touristy road as we were. I had to get him up here to the Empire State Building. I felt in a way, that's where it all began.

"Are you cold?" my dear husband asked of me, *my husband* for nearly four wonderful years. We married not long after finding each other again, no reason to wait.

Smoothing my hands down his arms, I absorbed him at my core, his arms strong and massive body wonderfully crowding me, keeping me warm and tight.

Keeping me safe.

Safety I'd never felt anything short of when it came to Blake Chandler and that safety went beyond the physical. I was literally *protected* by him in all the ways I could be. I was able to be who I wanted to be and enjoy the life *I* wanted to have. I didn't have to live up to anyone else's perceptions.

I'd done that long enough.

I started working at St. Albert's Hospital years ago in search of what I believed to be nothing at all. I worked at many hospitals up to that point, the life of a nurse my dream, but every opportunity and each new job assignment had never felt right. I was doing what I loved to do and living the way I wanted to live but never felt fulfilled. It wasn't until I got a surprise offer to move down to, of all places, Texas that things changed, the staff of a new hospital needed for its launch.

I wondered every day I set foot into work if he'd be there, the man who'd literally changed my life. I wondered if he was at the coffee house where I ventured to get my coffee or would suddenly appear where I filled up my Prius with gasoline. I wondered if we were passing ships in the night.

I wondered if he'd find me again.

Blake had a long road ahead of him after his heart attack but each day I was there for him, and after that initial kiss, I waited for him, expecting nothing but everything after that moment.

I said yes to his proposal the moment he'd asked.

We'd had a nice wedding at his local church, nothing like what my daddy had set up for my ex-husband and me. No, I hadn't even planned my own wedding back then, but this, being married to my soul mate...

We'd remember it forever. We'd remember it because it was us. It was small and special and perfect, his family there and even mine too. They came to Texas for my second wedding, the one that meant something because it was to someone who'd been my choice. He was mine forever.

And I was happily his.

I let Blake hold me, smiling when his lips brushed the shell of my ear. His whiskers tickling, I tried not to snicker beneath him. When he told me he sought to cut off his goatee and grow out a full beard, I hadn't known what I thought about that. I liked his facial hair and wasn't too keen on it changing. I supported him though and in the end was extremely happy with the decision he made.

The beard managed to make that man even sexier than he was.

I saw him before he kissed me, parting my lips open at the top of one of the largest buildings. We'd traveled to my home for a vacation, Valentine's Day.

"I could never be cold," I hummed against his lips, chilled from the wind up here. Pulling back, I cupped his face, those same blue eyes I fell in love with over thirty years ago.

He'd changed so much but not really. Work and time had changed him, made him older and harder around the eyes, but each day I saw that time leave, his expression and features anew with each passing day.

I hoped in my heart that had at least a little to do with me. I saw the same changes in myself in front of the bathroom mirror we shared in our country home. He released those same hardships... those same grips of life, which had me as well at one time, the time before him.

I brushed his blond whiskers. "I have you, you know?"

His eyes crinkled softly in the corners, his jaw moving before he pushed a hand beneath the blanket I had wrapped around my shoulders and to my hip.

He squeezed, placing his forehead against mine. We both did that a lot. In fact, every chance we got. It allowed us to center and connect, no words and only peaceful moments between us.

He danced me slowly to no music on the top of the Empire State Building, no sounds needed, and so lost in our euphoria we barely heard the young man asking to take our picture.

"I'm from the *Times*," he said to us, grinning behind a camera with a large flash above. "I'm capturing the couples up here on Valentine's Day, wanting to do a feature on them."

We both allowed it. Though, I knew Blake could be shy about these things. This still struck surprise in me since he was so large.

My big Teddy Bear.

I touched my forehead to his temple, our secret connection and the young man chose that moment to snap his shot, the light flashing around us in the setting evening. If we remembered in the morning we would gather that newspaper. I was sure his family would love to see it.

The boy thanked us, nodding his head before asking a final question.

"How long have you two been together?" he asked and I had a response right away, but Blake, well, he managed to beat me to it.

"Over thirty years," he said, his deep voice so lazy and handsome. Upon his lips touching my cheek, I smiled and the young man did the same.

"Major goals," he said to us, popping his camera up before pursuing a couple not far from us.

In his absence, Blake and I got back to where we were, not taking any moment for granted. We never did, each passing day one we held on to like the most valuable thing we could possibly have in our possession.

"You count the time away," I finally said to him, his arms around me as we stared out at the city ahead. We'd been here several times since we'd been married, as we visited my family a few times a year.

That was very important to Blake, family, and even though I had been a bit estranged from mine with the history we'd had in regard to the respect they had of my decisions from wanting to be a nurse to my ultimate divorce from my first husband, he urged me to fix those ties.

"We can't choose who they are," he'd said to me one night, the night we'd gotten married. "But we can be the ones to love, to love hard in spite of any and everything. We can be the example. We can be the best."

He'd been so right and I lived my life that way from that day, the best, the example and the one to love the hardest.

Closing my eyes, I waited for his voice. I always counted that time we were away from each other. I *always* had in my heart but had never said anything. I didn't know if I expected a drawback or something else entirely. I just hadn't taken the risk.

Touching my hand, Blake squeezed, turning me around to face him.

"You've always been mine, Anita," he said, though was hard pressed to keep my gaze. He could be the worst in the shyness department. His lips twisted into a smile. "It doesn't matter the time lost."

I felt the same way, touching his hand when his fingers reached to brush my cheek. We'd both been asked if we regretted our decisions in the past, if we could have a do-over and choose each other, would we? To that, Blake had answered that to deny our pasts meant we wouldn't have our current future, his family and even the connections I made in my life. I couldn't imagine my life without his beautiful children and grandchildren and that... well, that definitely made up for the time. I couldn't have children, which had been one of the sole reasons my previous husband had been unfaithful to me for many years. If I'd had children, I might not have found Blake again or gotten to be a part of the lives of some amazing men Blake had been blessed to raise. I loved my new family and cherished my husband even more for giving them to me.

No, things were supposed to be the way they turned out and Blake and I had our whole lives ahead of us still, all that wonderful time even without the moments in the middle...

We still had our wonderful end.

Click the link below to download book seven of The Found by You series!

Download on Amazon

www.ingramcontent.com/pod-product-compliance
Lightning Source LLC
Chambersburg PA
CBHW070519200726

48293CB00007B/2598